NEW HAVEN FREE PUB LIB

W9-BAI-016

MAY 1 5 1990
CHILDREN'S ROOM

HOLIDAY SECTION

NEW HAVEN PUBLIC LIBRARY

DATE DUE

FEB 25 1991	APR 18 1998	
MAR 2 8 1991	APR 17 1999	
APR 15 1991		
OCT 21 1991	MAY 02 2009	
APR 20 1992	APR 26 2010	
	APR 25 2011	
MAY 12 1992	APR 27 2012	
APR 13 1993	APR 15 2013	
APR 2 4 1995	APR 28 2014	
	MAR 30 2016	
APR 20 1996		
MAR 26 1997	APR 13 2016	
APR 04 1998		
MAY 01 2006		

MISS SUZY'S
EASTER SURPRISE

By Miriam Young

Pictures by Arnold Lobel

Aladdin Books
Macmillan Publishing Company
New York

Collier Macmillan Publishers
London

Text copyright © 1972 by Walter Young
Illustrations copyright © 1972 by Arnold Lobel
All rights reserved. No part of this book may be reproduced or
transmitted in any form or by any means, electronic or mechanical,
including photocopying, recording, or by any information storage
and retrieval system, without permission in writing from the
Publisher.

Four Winds Press
Macmillan Publishing Company
866 Third Avenue, New York, NY 10022
Collier Macmillan Canada, Inc.

Printed in the United States of America
Library of Congress Catalog Card Number: 80-16966

First Edition

10   9   8   7   6   5   4   3   2

Library of Congress Cataloging in Publication Data

Young, Miriam Burt.
    Miss Suzy's Easter surprise.

    Originally published by Parents' Magazine Press,
New York.
    SUMMARY: Miss Suzy, a squirrel, interrupts her
Easter preparations to become a temporary mother to four
little orphan squirrels.
    [1. Squirrels — Fiction. 2. Easter stories]
I. Lobel, Arnold, II. Title.
[PZ7.Y873Mj   1980]   [E]   80-16966
ISBN 0-02-793680-5

For Martha, with love

iss Suzy was as busy as a squirrel could be. She was getting ready for Easter.

On Saturday morning she gave her house a good cleaning, and as she worked she sang:

I'll never move, oh no, not I,
From my dear little home so near the sky.

In the afternoon she took out her recipe for a
special Easter cake:

> *1 cup ground acorns,*
> *½ cup maple seed,*
> *¼ cup of dew.*
> Mix well and bake until brown.

Miss Suzy mixed everything well and put the cake in the oven. When it was done she sat down to sew. She was making herself an Easter bonnet with a wide, floppy brim.

"There!" she said, when it was sewn together. "All it needs is some trimmings."

She scurried to a nearby hickory tree, for she had seen a piece of ribbon caught in its branches.

Just enough for my hat! Miss Suzy thought, pulling the ribbon from the branch. She put it in her bucket and sat looking around. She was fond of this hickory tree. It had fine nuts in the fall, but was too close to a road with noisy trucks and cars.

"I'm not fussy," said Miss Suzy, "but I do like quiet. Thank goodness for my lovely, peaceful oak."

It was a cloudy day, and now a drop of rain fell. Then another. Miss Suzy ran to the end of a branch and jumped to a maple tree. The grass at the foot of the maple was filled with fresh green clover. Miss Suzy picked enough for a wreath and sat looking around. The maple tree had nice seed pods in the spring, but lost its leaves early in the fall, while the big, papery leaves of her oak tree stayed on and on and on.

"I'm not fussy," said Miss Suzy, "but I do like to be dry and cozy. Thank goodness for my lovely, leafy oak."

Now it was raining lightly. Miss Suzy scampered up the maple and jumped down to a little willow tree that stood by a lake. At the water's edge were clusters of pink and blue forget-me-nots,

exactly the right size for her hat. Miss Suzy had
just gathered a bouquet when lightning flashed.
Thunder rumbled. The rain *poured* down.

Miss Suzy scurried up the willow tree and into a hole in the trunk. She peeped out. The willow had neither nuts nor seed pods, and its leaves were narrow. It had no view at all—for though the hole was spacious, the maple branches close by stretched over the smaller tree and blocked out the sky.

"I'm not fussy," said Miss Suzy, "but I couldn't go to sleep at night if I couldn't see the stars. Thank goodness, oh, thank goodness for my lovely, tall oak."

The storm grew worse. The willow wands were whipping in the wind. The top of the maple was thrashing about and the hickory was swaying. Miss Suzy knew that her oak tree stood firm as a rock—but she had left a window open!

Oh dear, she thought. My good moss carpet! I'd better get home!

But she could hardly move against the wind.
It blew right through her fur as she slowly
pushed on.

Then suddenly—*crack!* An old apple tree crashed down, its twigs splintering and snapping.

From the fallen tree there came a squeaking. Miss Suzy ran over to investigate. There in a broken branch were four little squirrels. Miss Suzy was so worried and upset she sounded cross.

"What are you doing here? Do you want to catch cold? You can't stay here. Where's your mother?"

The little squirrels were silent. They had no mother.

Miss Suzy didn't know what to do. There wasn't room for them in her little one-room house. Besides, they'd be soaking wet by the time she got them to the top of the tall oak tree.

"Come along," she said, and carrying the smallest, she led them to the hole in the little willow. It wasn't much of a house but it was roomy. And the children would be out of the rain. Miss Suzy put the littlest one down to nap on a bed of leaves and talked to the others quietly.

"We'll fix this place up as best we can. You can't go back to the apple tree."

When the rain stopped, she went with the two older squirrels to their old nest and brought back a few pieces of furniture. Then leaving them to arrange it, Miss Suzy scurried home.

Except for some acorn cups that had fallen from their hooks and a damp spot on her carpet, everything was fine. Miss Suzy quickly gathered up a supply of nuts and carried them to the house in the willow. Then, because she was so tidy herself, she made another trip to take them a little twig broom.

That evening Miss Suzy could scarcely keep her eyes open. She sewed the trimmings on her hat and crept into bed. She was very tired. But she had finished her hat, the sky was clear, and she could count a million stars.

The next morning Miss Suzy tried on her hat. Its wide brim was wreathed with clover. There were blue ribbons to tie under her chin and a bunch of forget-me-nots on one side. "It's the most beautiful hat in the world!" she cried. "I must pay a few calls and invite someone to the house for tea."

Miss Suzy was halfway out the door when she remembered the little squirrels. They'd have no Easter baskets, poor children! And where could she get Easter baskets now, on Sunday morning?

Miss Suzy stood for a moment in thought. Then she went in and took off her beautiful Easter bonnet. She cut it in half, cut each half in half again and folded the four pieces into baskets. She filled the baskets with acorns and cake, decorated them with forget-me-nots and tied ribbon bows on the handles.

Miss Suzy put on her old hat and ran to the willow.

The little squirrels were delighted to see her. And when they saw the Easter baskets, their eyes widened. They hadn't expected to get anything at all. Simon took her hat, Sylvester brought a chair for her to sit on, Serena dusted it off. And little Stevie brought her a beautiful pebble.

"Keep it," he said. "I want you to."

They were the nicest children she'd ever seen.

Miss Suzy had other calls to make, but it was hard to leave. The house needed so much attention, and so did the children. They ran about, chattering happily, while she mended their clothes and got their dinner. Later, they listened quietly while she told them stories and sang some songs. Before she knew it, the day was over. It was time to go.

"I'll come to see you again," said Miss Suzy.

The children were suddenly silent.

"I'll come back soon," she promised, "and bring you another cake."

The children just looked at her solemnly. Miss Suzy put on her hat and went to say good night to Stevie. He was already in his crib. He stood up. "You've got your hat on."

"Yes," said Miss Suzy, "I have to go now."
"I thought you were going to stay," said Stevie.
"No," said Miss Suzy, "I only came to visit. I have my own house to take care of."

"I thought you were going to stay," Stevie
repeated, "and be our mother."

Miss Suzy looked at his wide brown eyes. She
took off her hat. "Well," she said, "I am."

That night, when the children were asleep, Miss Suzy put her head out the hole. High in the oak tree, up near the stars, her little house stood empty, its firefly lamps twinkling through the dark. Some day, not very far off, the children would be able to take care of themselves and she could go home again.

Miss Suzy sighed. What a strange day it had
been—with no Easter calls, no guests for tea,
and no new bonnet. Then she looked down at
the lake.

There were the stars! They were reflected
in the dark surface of the water. And there was
the moon, too. It had been a wonderful Easter
after all.

MAY 1 1990